Inside

Chernobyl

A Day in the Exclusion Zone

© 2020 Chris Nagy

Chris Nagy

Katharinenstraße 25

73728 Esslingen am Neckar

Germany

contact@chrisnagy.de

Publishing and printing:

Amazon Media EU S.à r.l., 5 Rue Plaetis, L-2338, Luxembourg

1. Edition

Table of contents

WHY CHERNOBYL IS WORTH A VISIT 1

THE HISTORY OF THE CHERNOBYL NUCLEAR POWER PLANT 4

    THE CREATION OF THE POWER PLANT AND ITS TECHNICAL FEATURES 4
    THE NUCLEAR DISASTER ON APRIL 26, 1986 6
    CLEAN-UP AND CONSEQUENCES OF THE DISASTER 10
    THE CURRENT SITUATION IN THE EXCLUSION ZONE 14

OUR EXPLORATION OF THE EXCLUSION ZONE 17

    ORGANIZATION & ARRIVAL 17
    THE RIDE TO DYTYATKY CHECKPOINT 21
    THE ABANDONED VILLAGE OF SALESJE 23
    WALK THROUGH THE CITY OF CHERNOBYL 28
    THE KINDERGARTEN OF KOPACHI 36
    EXPLORING THE GHOST TOWN OF PRIPYAT 40
    LUNCH BREAK IN THE CHERNOBYL CANTEEN 50
    THE SARCOPHAGUS ABOVE THE DAMAGED REACTOR CORE 51
    THE DEPARTURE FROM THE EXCLUSION ZONE 53

A DAY IN THE CHERNOBYL EXCLUSION ZONE - MY PERSONAL
CONCLUSION 56

BONUS CHAPTER: THE SECRET RADAR STATION DUGA-1 62

FREQUENTLY ASKED QUESTIONS (FAQ) 65

Why Chernobyl is worth a visit

On April 26, 1986, the Chernobyl nuclear disaster was the first event to be assigned to the highest level according to the seven-level international rating scale for nuclear and radiological events. Several trillion becquerels of radioactive substances were released during this catastrophic accident, which is approximately 900 times more than the Hiroshima atomic bomb. The consequences of the explosion of reactor 4 brought unbelievable suffering to the population living there. Thousands died from the late effects of the catastrophe. Hundreds of thousands lost their homes, their economic existence and now have to live with the mental and psychosocial consequences of the disaster. An area of 1,000 mi^2 will probably not be able to be used by humans for hundreds of years.

Should one really visit this place for vacation?

Among friends and relatives, the announcement of our intention to travel to Chernobyl was initially received very differently. Probably, the largest group of people informed in advance were seriously concerned about our well-being. In public perception, Chernobyl is still considered a life-threatening place, inaccessible to humans. Terms from the media such as "death zone" feed the rumors that visitors must be tired of life. Various inquiries followed, whether we had thought it over well and whether we were aware of possible consequences. Others expressed incomprehension of our plans and could not understand the reasons for a visit. There are so many beautiful places on our planet, why travel to a place with such a tragic history? They also couldn't quite understand what was so appealing about the ruins of an abandoned city. Lastly, there were those who perhaps would not trust themselves to make such a trip but were looking forward with us to the experiences ahead. After all, we would be visiting a place that most people only knew from television or computer games.

Primarily, the following three reasons moved me to make a trip to Chernobyl:

1. A trip to Chernobyl is something special: even though the number of visitors is growing year by year, only a tiny fraction of the population has ever visited the place. So, if you decide to take a tour through the exclusion zone, you can be almost certain that no one in your circle of friends has been there before you. Tense listeners are, therefore, practically guaranteed to hear the stories of your experiences after you return home.
2. Staying in the exclusion zone is a real adventure: restricted military area, ghost towns, dilapidated ruins, wild animals, and above everything lies the uncertain danger of invisible radiation. There is hardly any other place in the world where a visit is so exciting, varied, and interesting at the same time. The fact that for many people, the mere thought of visiting Chernobyl gives them

an eerie feeling makes the trip even more attractive from an adventurer's point of view.

3. Visiting the historical sites makes history tangible: Most people are familiar with the historical events surrounding the Chernobyl nuclear accident. Nevertheless, it is difficult to imagine what exactly happened at that time, how the local people experienced the nuclear disaster, and how the environment developed after the catastrophe. Seeing the places of the events with our own eyes helps to bring the historical events to life for us personally. The events of Chernobyl are an inseparable part of the history of industrialization and have had a lasting impact on European politics. The victims of the disaster and the lessons learned from it should therefore not be forgotten.

The travelogue is intended for adventurers who are also planning to visit Chernobyl and those who can't imagine visiting but still want the first-hand experience. So, you will hear about all the discoveries we made during our tour in Chernobyl, what we experienced while visiting these unique places and how we felt about it. In addition, you will learn everything you need to know about traveling to the exclusion zone. Our experiences are always put into the historical context, so that experience and history will merge in a meaningful way. Numerous pictures of the most exciting places give you the feeling of having been there.

The history of the Chernobyl nuclear power plant

The creation of the power plant and its technical features

In order to be able to meet the growing energy needs of the Soviet Union in the long term, it was decided in 1970 to build the first nuclear power plant on the territory of today's Ukraine. While initially only two reactors were planned for the power plant near the district town of Chernobyl, during construction, the planning was expanded to a total of six reactor units. During its operation, the power plant supplied up to 10% of Ukraine's required electricity and was thus of great importance in terms of energy policy.

To provide housing for the workers and employees and their families, a new city was specially designed and built. In the 1970s and 1980s, the modern city of Pripyat developed into one of the places with the highest standard of living in the Soviet Union. A perfect supply of goods, a flourishing retail trade, and a rich cultural offer benefited not only the mainly by young families but also attracted tourists and vacationers who wanted to contemplate the new way of life in the Soviet Union. The Chernobyl nuclear power plant, which was to employ up to 10,000 workers after completing the six reactors, was the primary employer and the city's pride.

The technical basis for the nuclear power plant was provided by RBMK-1000 reactors, which are graphite-moderated. For the controlled nuclear fission of uranium atoms, the neutrons responsible for the chain reaction must be slowed down. The moderator used for this purpose in this type of reactor is not water, as is usually the case, but graphite. The fuel rods with the enriched uranium and the water-cooling system are located in numerous pressure tubes in the graphite blocks. The thermal energy generated during nuclear fission is absorbed by the cooling water. The resulting steam is in turn used in steam turbines to drive generators and thus produce electrical power. So-called control rods control the nuclear chain reaction in the reactor. These are inserted into the reactor core from above to regulate power and cause the reactor to shut down when it is completely depressurized. This is usually done during operation with the aid of an automatic control system.

The power plant was considered a model plant in the Soviet Union in the 1980s. The disadvantages of the RBMK reactors due to their design only became apparent later. The control system of the reactors of this type is very sluggish, which makes a quick shutdown as a countermeasure to unforeseen events impossible. The control rods, which are fully extended under full load, take up to 20 seconds before they are fully retracted, resulting in reactor shutdown. In addition, unlike water-moderated reactors, a loss of coolant does not automatically lead to a loss of moderator, which interrupts the chain reaction. Due to the positive void coefficient of graphite-moderated reactors, reactivity actually increases when the diminishing coolant is heated, which can lead to a core meltdown. This misfortune is intensified by the fact that graphite is flammable and ignites under the heat of an impending core meltdown.

The nuclear disaster on April 26, 1986

Even a shutdown nuclear power plant depends on a supply of electrical energy to maintain its cooling system and to monitor its equipment and instruments. Normally, the shutdown power plant then draws its own requirements from the public power grid. If the grid is unavailable due to a large-scale power outage, emergency generators start up after a short ramp-up phase.

At the Chernobyl nuclear power plant on April 25, 1986, a test was to be carried out on unit 4 to determine whether, in the event of a power failure, whether the remaining rotational energy of the outgoing turbines would produce enough electricity to bridge the interim period until the emergency power generators were started up. The reactor was scheduled to continue operating at a lower power level for the duration of the test while the emergency cooling system and other safety systems were shut down. The crew was already beginning to lower the power level when the test had to be postponed until nighttime because an unforeseen power demand on the grid prevented the reactor from being further throttled back. During this waiting period, the reactor continued to operate at the throttled level for hours, contrary to the provisions of the operating manual. After every power reduction, this increased the concentration of the xenon-135 isotope, which, by imposing neutrons, reduces the reactivity of the reactor and thus its efficiency. In addition, the emergency cooling system remained switched off in the meantime, contrary to safety regulations.

Shortly after 11 p.m., preparations for the test were resumed by the now freshly arrived night shift. The night shift workers had been surprised by the postponed test and had not been trained on the test procedure in advance. Nevertheless, they continued with the test procedure as instructed and began to ramp down the reactor's power to about 25 percent. Suddenly, the power dropped precipitously to just 1 percent for reasons that have not yet been explained. A so-called xenon poisoning occurred, in which the concentration of xenon-135 increased so much that the nuclear chain reaction was stalled. Under normal circumstances, reactor operation may only be safely resumed one to two days after xenon poisoning, as soon as the xenon-135 concentration has decreased again through natural decay.

At this point, the next gross mistake of the day happened. The test director wanted to complete the test at any cost. Therefore, the team began to drive the control rods almost completely out of the reactor to increase reactivity again immediately and thus restart the nuclear chain reactions. Due to the still high concentration of xenon-135, the power remained at a level far too low for operation, only 7 percent of operating power, despite being set at full load. Nevertheless, the experiment continued.

When the valves of the turbine were then closed for the actual test, thus the heat removal from the reactor was interrupted, the effects that ultimately led to the power excursion of the reactor accumulated. The lack of heat removal caused the coolant to heat up, resulting in an increase in power due to the positive void coefficient. The increased power dissipated the crippling xenon poisoning, which in turn led to an increase in power. As reactivity increased, larger and larger amounts of vapor bubbles were created, increasing the power again.

Because of the uncontrolled power increase, the crew in the control room could do nothing but activate the AZ-5 manual emergency shutdown. This quick shutdown retracts the extended control rods, which usually ends the chain reaction. However, the RBMK reactors had another design flaw that has not been mentioned before and, for cost reasons, was not revised until the disaster. The tip of the Boron control rods was made of graphite, which increased power briefly when the control rods were retracted before decreasing as planned. As a result, the reactor, which was already at the edge of its capacity, exceeded one hundred times its rated value within fractions of a second. The first fuel rods exploded. The retracting control rods deformed and were thus unable to reach their final position in the reactor core. The superheated steam reacted with the Graphite and Zirconium from the cladding of the fuel rods. The resulting hydrogen and carbon monoxide escaped from the damaged reactor core and formed an explosive mixture of oxyhydrogen and water-gas with the oxygen in the reactor building. The mixture ignited and led to another explosion only seconds after the nuclear power excursion.

The explosion destroyed the lid of the reactor core, which weighed over 2,200,000 lbs, and the roof of the reactor building above it. This exposed the glowing reactor core without protection. Due to the contact with the atmosphere, the reactor core immediately caught fire. The explosion and the smoke from the subsequent fire released huge amounts of radioactive material and threw it into the air. Heavy soot and dust particles settled in the immediate surroundings of the nuclear power plant. The dangerous aerosols of highly volatile substances such as Iodine or Cesium reached heights of up to 6.2 miles due to the great heat of the graphite fire. From there, they spread as radioactive clouds, first over large parts of Europe and finally over the entire northern hemisphere. Alternating air currents drove them first to Scandinavia, then over Poland, today's Czech Republic, Austria, southern Germany to northern Italy. Another cloud reached the Balkans, Greece, and Turkey. The radiation exposure in the individual countries depended on whether the cloud passed over them or whether radiation particles reached the ground from the atmosphere through incipient rain.

Of the nearly 440,000 lbs of radioactive material contained in the reactor core, approximately 14,800 lbs escaped into the environment in the first ten days after the disaster. The half-life of the released radionuclides varied from a few days, which led to the acute radiation exposure on-site, to several thousand years, which still ensures that the area around the accident site will not be usable for humans in the long term.

The operators in the control room about 130 ft away were not injured by the explosion itself due to the thick concrete walls. However, the air contaminated with radioactive particles caused them to reach life-threatening radiation doses. Although the extent of the disaster should have been immediately clear to the experts on-site, the power plant management initially reported that there had only been a fire. They insisted on the opinion that the reactor was intact until the following evening.

Clean-up and consequences of the disaster

The alarmed firefighters first tried to extinguish the burning reactor core and the fires in the area around the accident site with cooling water. When it became clear that this alone would not be enough to contain the consequences of the disaster, military helicopters were used to fill the burning reactor core with shielding material from a height of over 650 ft. A total of 11 million pounds of material was brought and dropped from the reactor in around 1,800 helicopter flights. Boron carbide to stop the nuclear chain reaction; Dolomite to suppress the graphite; fire, sand, and clay to filter the radioactive materials; and Lead to shield the gamma radiation and seal the reactor core. Only when the reactor was cooled with Nitrogen more than ten days later, the fire was under control.

According to official figures, almost 50 people died as a result of acute radiation sickness. In this case, severe sickness and an attack of weakness occur within a few minutes. Other possible consequences are burns of the skin, the formation of tumors, and hair loss. After a phase of supposed recovery lasting several days, the dying phase follows, which is initiated by the death of the gastrointestinal tract and leads to massive diarrhea and intestinal bleeding. This is followed by severe fever, acute states of confusion, coma, and finally, death from circulatory failure. Treatment aims only to make the dying process more bearable for the patient.

By withholding information and downplaying the seriousness of the situation, it took a full 37 hours for Pripyat's 44,000 residents to be evacuated from the city after the accident. Thanks to the favorable wind flow towards less populated parts of the country, Pripyat did not suffer even more drastic consequences. Less than a week later, another 116,000 people from the area with a radius of about 18 miles around the reactor were taken out of the danger zone. In the following years, the number of resettled people increased to about 350,000.

A total of about 800,000 people assisted in the clean-up. These helpers were called liquidators because they were supposed to liquidate the consequences of the accident. Most of them were not aware that they were putting their lives in danger by working on the open reactor core.

1: The Chernobyl liquidators

One of the first tasks of the liquidators was to clear the roof of the neighboring third reactor unit from the highly radiated debris. This was to prevent the further spread of the radiation particles in the surrounding area. Due to the extremely high radiation levels, they were only allowed to stay on the roof for 45 seconds. This was just enough time to throw down a shovel of debris before they had to hurry back to the exit. The workers were inadequately equipped relative to the danger. Some of them, faced with the dire situation, wanted to do more than the few seconds allowed and stayed on the roof longer than agreed. In some cases, the recovery from the consequences of radiation sickness took several months. Several of them died in the course of the year.

In addition to clearing debris, liquidators helped build a tunnel to prevent contaminated firewater from seeping into the groundwater beneath the reactor. Others removed contaminated soil, cleaned roads, and buildings, cleared the radio-contaminated forests, or killed sick animals. But also, doctors, teachers, cooks, scientists, and translators gave their all in the following months to contain the consequences of the disaster.

With the first containment, hastily constructed in the months following the disaster, becoming increasingly leaky in the years that followed, construction of a new protective shell began in late 2010. The shell, known as the New Safe Confinement, was designed to last 100 years. During that time, it is intended to limit any radiation effects on the staff and the environment and limit the spread of radioactive contamination. Within the protective shell, the remains of the old sarcophagus will be gradually removed and the reactor dismantled. More than 40 countries were involved in the financing, which amounted to more than 2 billion euros.

Even today, people in the affected regions in Ukraine and Belarus suffer from the consequences of radioactive contamination. Compared to the time before the disaster, serious illnesses are increasing among the population. Diseases of the thyroid gland are persistent. The cancer rate has increased 30 times. There is no definitive agreement among experts on the number of deaths since the connection between long-lasting radiation doses, and the resulting diseases can only be proven statistically to a limited extent. However, according to a study by the anti-nuclear physicians' organization

"International Physicians for the Prevention of Nuclear War" (IPPNW), 112,000 of the 800,000 liquidators alone died as a result of their work. In addition to cancer, the population from the areas around Chernobyl suffers above all from social and psychological trauma.

Last but not least, the regional disaster in Chernobyl also changed the view of nuclear energy worldwide. Countries' reactions ranged from silence about the accident and its possible consequences to broad-based information campaigns about rules of behavior and protective measures for the population and increased controls in their own nuclear power plants to political efforts to abolish nuclear energy.

The current situation in the exclusion zone

Since Ukraine continued to rely on the Chernobyl nuclear power plant for economic and energy policy reasons, however, the undamaged units 1, 2, and 3 remained in operation even after reactor 4 was destroyed in the wake of the nuclear disaster on April 26, 1986. However, they were upgraded with elaborate safety measures, including installing a true fast shutdown to prevent another disaster. The remaining units were finally taken off the grid one by one between 1991 and 2000 under pressure from the European Union, following several extensions of their operating licenses. Construction work on units 5 and 6, which had not been completed at the time of the disaster, continued initially. However, due to the high radioactive contamination of the area, these had to be stopped in 1988. The plan to continue them after the radiation had subsided was abandoned by

Ukraine as the successor state with the disintegration of the Soviet Union.

Reactor unit	Thermal power	Start of operation	Time of shutdown
Chernobyl-1	3,200 MW	27.05.1978	30.11.1996
Chernobyl-2	3,200 MW	28.05.1979	11.10.1991
Chernobyl-3	3,200 MW	08.06.1982	15.12.2000
Chernobyl-4	3,200 MW	26.03.1984	26.04.1986 (destroyed)
Chernobyl-5		Construction stopped in 1988	
Chernobyl-6		Construction stopped in 1988	

Pripyat is still completely abandoned today and forms the center of the exclusion zone as a ghost town. In Chernobyl, on the other hand, many buildings have been renovated. They now serve as accommodation for the workers and engineers who are still in the exclusion zone for maintenance and clean-up work and the soldiers, police officers, and firefighters.

In addition, several hundred illegal settlers, the so-called "samosely" (translated roughly as self-settlers), continue to live on the territory of the exclusion zone in Ukraine and Belarus. These are mainly elderly people who either refused to leave their homes during the evacuation or have since returned.

Since the middle of the 2010s, tourism has also found its way to Chernobyl. Day trips from Kiev are frequently used. The government of Ukraine announced its intention to increase the number of tourists from 60,000 annually to one million.

Our exploration of the exclusion zone

Organization & Arrival

If you are also curious and would like to see the historical sites of the disaster with your own eyes, there are some things you should consider before you start your trip to the Chernobyl exclusion zone. A self-organized trip to Chernobyl is not allowed for tourists, and from our point of view, it is not recommended at all. The Chernobyl exclusion zone is several hundred square miles in size, and there are still many dangers lurking in this area, especially for people without sufficient local knowledge.

However, there are now numerous offers from travel agencies on the Internet that can help you with your project. When organizing this adventure, it was vital for us to choose a professional provider who would organize the necessary permits for entering the restricted area and give us the feeling that he would also bring us home again safely and without any consequential damage.

After a short research, we decided on the provider CHORNOBYL TOUR (www.chernobyl-tour.com). In addition to various military and underground tours in Kiev, they also offer one-day and multi-day tours to the Chernobyl exclusion zone. We booked the classic one-day tour in English for $99, which would take us to the following places, among others:

- the abandoned village of Salesje

- the town of Chernobyl with the fire station from which the emergency forces first arrived at the scene of the accident
- the abandoned kindergarten of Kopachi
- the town of Prypyat with its famous amusement park, the empty swimming pool, and the devastated school
- the large square within sight of the new containment above the accident reactor
- the secret military radar facility Duga-1

In addition to the cost of the organized tour, you should add some budget for worthwhile additional options. The lunch in the exclusion zone for an extra $8 later became an interesting experience. Touched by the first impressions, we had our meal together with the workers and administrators still working in the exclusion zone in the Chernobyl canteen.

Also recommended is a Geiger counter, which we could borrow for a fee of $10. With the help of this device, it is possible to measure the invisible, tasteless and odorless radiation. It was only when the radiation was shown that we really became aware of the ever-present danger. Furthermore, it offered the opportunity to search for evidence even more intensively and compare the different locations at different distances from the accident reactor.

Following the booking, the agency took care of the official registration and all permits necessary to enter the restricted area with the help of our passport data.

2: *The location of the Chernobyl exclusion zone*

The Chernobyl nuclear power plant is located in northern Ukraine. Europe's second-largest country by area bordered Russia to the east and was part of the Soviet Union until its disintegration in 1991. Due to the winds blowing north at the time of the disaster, which dispersed the nuclear particles, the nuclear exclusion zone extends to the neighboring territories of Belarus to the north. However, the part that is open for inspection lies entirely within Ukraine.

The starting point of our trip to Chernobyl was, therefore, the city of Kiev, about 95 miles away, which is also the capital of Ukraine. It can be easily reached internationally via Kiev-Boryspil Airport or the much smaller Kiev-Schuljany Airport. It has numerous connections to Eastern and Western Europe and the Middle and Near East, such as Russia, Kazakhstan, Georgia, Iran, Turkey, Poland, Italy, Germany, Denmark, Sweden, Great Britain, France, Portugal, Austria, and Israel. Long-haul connections are currently offered to China, India, Dubai, Canada, and the East Coast of the United States.

3: View over Kiev

Kiev is a lively city with its rich culture and centuries-old history and is suitable for a long weekend at any time of the year. Especially the impressive architecture of the Orthodox churches, with their golden domes in the monastery complexes and the beautiful house facades around the Maidan Square, are inviting for an extensive city walk. Both the streets and the parks are very clean and make a well-kept impression. The varied Ukrainian cuisine, which is closely related to Russian cuisine, invites you to try and feast. Especially the delicious soups, stews, and dumplings are very popular far beyond the country's borders. Due to the decreased value of the Ukrainian currency Hryvnia, Ukraine represents a favorable travel destination from the point of view of travelers from Western countries. For a generous 3-course meal, for example, we paid only the equivalent of $22.

The ride to Dytyatky checkpoint

It is still dark when we reach the meeting point for our tour in the heart of Kiev at 07:30 a.m. on a cold day in December. A minibus with the inscription CHORNOBYL TOUR behind the windshield is already waiting for us. Our guide, Kateryna, welcomes us in a friendly manner and briefly checks that each participant is carrying his or her passport. Without it, it is impossible to enter the restricted zone. It is a matter of course for us to wear long clothing and closed shoes in the Ukrainian winter when we expect temperatures as low as 5 °F. With a small group of twelve people from five different countries, we set off on the journey from Kiev to one of the official border posts of the restricted zone.

For the historical classification of the places, we would visit in the course of the day, a documentary about the nuclear disaster is shown on a large screen in the minibus. It describes the course of the accident and the subsequent clean-up efforts. Shocking original footage of the debris and people injured and eyewitness accounts from surviving helpers give us a rough idea of the destructive energy that can be unleashed by nuclear fission and the inconceivable suffering this catastrophe has caused among the population. For a brief moment, I doubt our intention to visit this grim place as part of a vacation. On the other hand, a visit is also instructive. The disaster is now also an integral part of the history of industrialization, in which humans tried to use nuclear power for their own benefit. Chernobyl has now become a memorial to the victims and heroes of those days. Without the courageous efforts of the helpers in the hours and days following the accident, the catastrophe would have had far more severe consequences for all mankind. The mood on the bus is tense in view of the film footage. Every single person is eager to see what they were supposed to see today and excited about the uncertain adventure we are about to embark on.

After about two hours of driving, we reach a roadblock. The bus stops, we get out and have our passports ready for inspection. Kateryna points out to us once again that filming or photographing military buildings is prohibited. On the left, a large sign in Cyrillic and Latin script with the nuclear radiation symbol sticking out lets us know that we are about to enter a radioactively contaminated zone. Ukrainian authorities will prosecute any unauthorized entry. On the right side, there is a small building, obviously used for administration. Ukrainian militia officers armed with Russian machine guns control the observance of the rules. Kateryna registers us in the small administration building and gets our passports checked. After a short examination by the militia, we are allowed to get back into our minibus and pass the gate to the restricted area.

We have now arrived at a place where we are not supposed to be and where, since the catastrophe of 1986, no one should be; Completely voluntarily and out of our own conviction.

The abandoned village of Salesje

The first stop of the day is a small village on the edge of the exclusion zone. Here we are still in the moderate part within the 18 miles radius around the accident reactor. A narrow road leads us to a small settlement, which comprises no more than two or three houses and lies on the edge of a forest area. The snow is still untouched. We are allowed to get out of the car and first examine the abandoned houses from a distance. The area reminds me of a small allotment garden settlement. The houses are single-story and not very large, but a small garden surround each. Around the property, you can still see the remains of a dilapidated fence. Apart from our group, no one is around.

4: Abandoned house in Salesje

We now have the opportunity to look around independently on foot and explore with our Geiger counters. Kateryna warns us to be careful because the old buildings are now badly damaged by decades of vacancy, and parts of the floors have already collapsed. From the outside, the buildings still make a relatively good impression at first glance. The roof is still intact, as far as can be judged from the snow. The front is dry. Only the windows have been partially broken in or completely dismantled. Slowly, we approach the first house.

A closer look inside the building reveals the traces of time. The blue paint on the brick interior walls has already peeled off in places. Tiles that have fallen off and cracked bear witness to the fact that the walls in some rooms must have been covered with tiles. A high layer of dust lies over everything. The floor is still intact; there are the remains of wooden parts, tiles, crumbled plaster, scraps of paper, and broken bottles. In other places, the wooden floor is no longer there at all, and you can see down to the dirt floor between the large wooden beams on which the house stands. There is enough light coming in through the windows that you could see the scenery very well in daylight. You wouldn't want to be here in the dark anyway, as the atmosphere is already spooky enough in full daylight and in a group. We move carefully along the beams and wood scraps through the house. We remind each other to be careful not to slip or break through at an unsecured spot. We cautiously investigate each new room with a queasy feeling, with the shuddering thought of encountering a stranger who might take offense at our unwanted intrusion. Empty bottles and two old mattresses make it seem as if the house was still partially used as a shelter after the evacuation. Besides dirt and junk, we find no other personal belongings. Most of the inventory seems to have been looted from the houses left behind long before our time.

5: Destroyed furnishings in the abandoned houses

We go outside again and make our way to the second house. In the process, we notice the deflection on the measurement display of our Geiger counters for the first time. At the edge of the exclusion zone, the radiation is still very low so that the device itself remains silent. We compare the measurement results from different places and notice that the radiation intensity is quite different. While we can measure almost no radiation on the roadways, the radiation increases progressively at the roadside and in the direction of the forest. At so-called hotspots, a place with permanently strong radiation, it even increases in leaps over time. On average, we measure values of 0.18 microsieverts per hour in Salesje, which is quite comparable to the natural radiation in many cities on earth. In Germany, for example, the natural radiation level is 0.24 microsieverts per hour. For us, the idea that radiation in what is often called the "death zone" should be more harmless than in one of the safest countries in the world is initially astonishing. But we are only at the beginning of our journey.

The second house we visit already offers more. It is littered with old scraps of paper, newspaper remains, old books, and handwritten notes. Not all the rooms are walk-in because this time, you can't look through the carpet to see if any broken-in places are lurking underneath. Some of the walls have been pried open as if someone was looking for something behind them. Doors are virtually non-existent throughout the house, with only the remains of a door frame still lying around in the back.

We find a book in which someone had neatly written down a list of names. The book is in perfect condition in relation to the rest of the inventory, giving rise to the suspicion that it may have been left behind intentionally as some sort of exhibit. Suddenly we are startled to see a small sinister figure in the corner of our eye. What we see, however, turns out to be an orphaned child doll. Nevertheless, this sight remains in our memory, as it perfectly describes the eerie atmosphere of this place.

On the way back to the minibus, we continue looking for hotspots. Even though it sounds almost absurd in retrospect, we were all the more excited, the higher the values turned out to be. We try to outdo each other with peak values. One of our fellow travelers finds a gas mask half-covered by the snow. Such supposedly accidental finds drive up the excitement of the group once again. However, just as with the book or the doll, we are not quite sure whether we are dealing with a relic of old times or a cleverly placed gimmick intended to impress the tourists.

Walk through the city of Chernobyl

We continue to the city of Chernobyl. Although the name Chernobyl is initially associated mainly with the nuclear power plant, the city of the same name is located about 11 miles from the accident site. Thus, it is still within the exclusion zone but outside the 6 miles core zone. The most famous pictures around the exclusion zone, on the other hand, were taken in the town of Pripyat, right next to the nuclear reactors.

The city itself looks back on a history of more than 800 years, in which the city in different epochs already belonged to Ukraine, Lithuania and Poland, was occupied by Germany during the Second World War and after the dissolution of the Soviet Union, is now again part of Ukraine. The city became famous in its history mainly for the production of iron and its forged products. At the entrance to the city, the stone town sign awaits us, emblazoned with the name Chernobyl in Cyrillic letters. The red hammer and sickle date back to the Soviet era. The ornaments recall the long-forgotten golden age of the city with its factories and its port for steamships on the banks of the Dnipro River.

6: Chernobyl town sign

Before the disaster, Chernobyl had about 14,000 inhabitants, who were evacuated a full nine days after the accident. Today, about 1,000 people still live in the town, most of them working on-site as maintenance or administrative staff around the nuclear power plant. Chernobyl has been largely renovated for this purpose and, unlike the other towns in the exclusion zone, is in good condition. It even has its own hotel. In addition, there are still a few returnees living here who are in the area illegally but are largely tolerated by the authorities. For the most part, they are people who were discriminated against outside the restricted area because of their origin and had no other perspective than to continue living on the land on which they had grown up. In addition, some older people could not imagine a new start away from their hometown. These people live on local produce, which increases the exposure of the illegal settlers relative to the employees who obtain their food from outside the restricted zone. During our trip through the restricted area, we did not meet any of these self-settlers. The announcement of the travel agency that we would be able to meet and talk to one of the self-supporters did not come true, as the lady could not be found at that time. Her fate remained unknown to us but obviously could be a move due to illness or the death of the illegal settler.

As we leave the bus, a large group of wild dogs is streaming towards us. The entire tour group backs away in fear of being attacked or bitten. The pack surrounds us and approaches purposefully. Our guide Kateryna, however, remains relaxed. Relieved, we notice that the strays make a peaceful impression and probably only expect a bite to eat from the visitors. From the color of their fur, we realize that they must be a diverse group of different breeds of dogs. Despite their wildlife, they are well fed and seem to be fit and lively. Some of them are even pretty to look at. In the dog lovers immediately arises the desire to pet, cuddle or play with the four-legged friends. We quickly wipe this thought aside because we were in the Chernobyl exclusion zone, and nobody knows what dangerous substances the dogs are exposed to by living in a nuclear contaminated area. Even though it almost breaks our hearts, we try to avoid the dogs as much as possible and continue exploring on foot.

We first pass a large field where hundreds of crosses are placed in two long rows. The names of people who died here due to the reactor accident are inscribed on the crossbars in Cyrillic characters. The sight at first reminds me of a military cemetery, as they were built after the First and Second World War. Instead of white crosses on a green meadow, we look at black, scrawny steel crosses in Chernobyl, which stick out of the snow on a foggy gray December day in the dreary surroundings.

A few hundred feet further, we reach a steel statue built in a similar style. The huge depicted angel is certainly 50 ft high and consists of constructions of many individual forged steel struts. He holds a large trombone in his hands, stretched out wide, and blows into it firmly.

7: Monument of the Third Angel

The statue bears the meaningful name "Monument of the Third Angel" and is dedicated to the fallen firefighters and emergency workers of the nuclear disaster. The name is based on a Bible verse from the Revelation of John, which, as part of the prophetic visions of the Apocalypse, is about this same angel:

"And the third angel sounded,
and there fell a great star from Heaven, burning as it were a lamp,
and it fell upon the third part of the rivers,
and upon the fountains of waters;

> And the name of the star is called Wormwood:
> and the third part of the waters became wormwood;
> and many men died of the waters because they were made bitter."

Some contemporary witnesses even feared that the Chernobyl disaster had already been predetermined in the Bible and that the catastrophe now heralded the end of the world. The emergency forces themselves, by the way, did not know anything about the nuclear disaster at the time they were alerted. They thought it was an ordinary fire and a routine operation. However, those who were deployed directly at the open reactor and were fighting the toxic flames there noticed the catastrophic effects of the high doses of radioactive emissions directly in their own bodies. Their skin burned and blistered due to the high radiation exposure. The immune system struggled to cope with the effects of the radiation, with the bone marrow working at full capacity to produce infection-fighting white blood cells. The circulatory system eventually collapsed from exhaustion. Twenty-nine people died of acute radiation sickness in the days after the disaster, and hundreds more fell ill in the coming weeks as they tried to avert an even greater catastrophe. With the horrific thoughts of decomposition from radiation sickness, we continue our journey through Chernobyl.

Half an hour later, we finally reach the main Chernobyl fire station. The site consists of several buildings, another memorial, and a fenced-off area where the historic vehicles that had assisted in fighting the fire are lined up. The fire station itself makes a well-kept impression.

It is surrounded by an orange wall and has an ornate entrance gate with blue pipes, gold bracing, and a large logo. Two simple red-and-white emergency vehicles stand ready for action in the courtyard. The fire station is still manned and operating at the time of our visit. The door to the gatehouse is open. If you didn't know that you were currently in the restricted military area, you could easily have mistaken it for a typical fire station somewhere in an Eastern European village.

8: Monument to Those Who Saved The Word

The memorial in front of the fire station called the "Monument to Those Who Saved The World" shows a troop of firefighters at work. Those pictured to the left and right of the pillar are clearing debris, carrying fire hoses, and using radiation detectors to search for contaminated debris. The fellows support each other, help stumbling colleagues back to their feet, and carry injured colleagues away from the source of danger. The monument is dedicated not only to the firefighters but also to the so-called liquidators, who took over the clean-up work during the accident and in its aftermath. This group of people of clean-up and repair workers included, in addition to those who directly participated in the removal of the debris, those who helped in the removal of the contaminated soil, in the cleaning of roads, buildings, forests, and equipment, and in the construction and building of the sarcophagus to shield the reactor core exposed by the explosion.

Furthermore, the group of liquidators included many other professionals such as doctors, teachers, cooks, and translators who worked in the contaminated exclusion zone. In total, it is estimated that between 600,000 and 800,000 workers, including scientists, miners, and military personnel, were involved in the clean-up efforts around Chernobyl. Knowing about the unbelievable historical events, even this ordinary statue, makes us speechless and thoughtful.

On the opposite side of the area, cordoned off by a small fence with signs indicating particularly high levels of radioactive contamination, are several historic salvage vehicles and robots. The exhibit features a wide variety of vehicles, ranging from small wheel loaders and mini excavators painted in blue, yellow and red, to remote-controlled search robots and large armored vehicles with room for several passengers. After the disaster, when those responsible became aware of how incredibly strong the radiation and how contaminated the debris and material to be removed were, the clean-up work should be made less hazardous for the people involved. For this purpose, it was decided to use unmanned vehicles. Countries such as Japan and Germany willingly provided their own recovery robots. Since the real extent of the radiation released was classified as a state secret and withheld from the foreign technicians and engineers, the project was doomed to failure from the start. On-site, the radiation turned out to be so strong that all vehicles in use failed to operate within a very short time. Due to the radiation, the circuits of the electronics simply burned out.

Compared to the village of Salesje, the radiation at the edge of the cordoned-off recovery vehicles here in the second radius of the exclusion zone is already three times as high, with peaks of up to 6.6 microsieverts per hour. Even though we find it astonishing that after a relatively long period of time of three decades, the consequences can still be measured, the duration is only a blink of an eye from the point of view of the half-life of the radioactive material plutonium-239 with more than 24,000 years. And so, the region will probably have to live with the consequences of the catastrophe for many thousands of years to come.

The kindergarten of Kopachi

Driving towards the disaster reactor and the heart of the exclusion zone, we now reach the village of Kopachi. Due to the wind direction during the disaster, the village was hit particularly hard by the radiation. Therefore, it was decided to demolish almost all buildings in the village. However, contrary to expectations, this had the negative effect that the radioactive isotopes were able to penetrate deeper into the soil via the groundwater and thus spread further. At the time of our visit, the kindergarten and a statue from the Second World War are still there.

After the small houses in Salesje, we have now with just this kindergarten for the first time again the possibility to visit a building from the inside. Time has also left its mark on the kindergarten. The paint is peeling off in large parts of the building, wetness is spreading from broken pipes in the walls, leaves have blown into the rooms through the broken and open windows, and books and paper pages are scattered on the dusty and dirty floors.

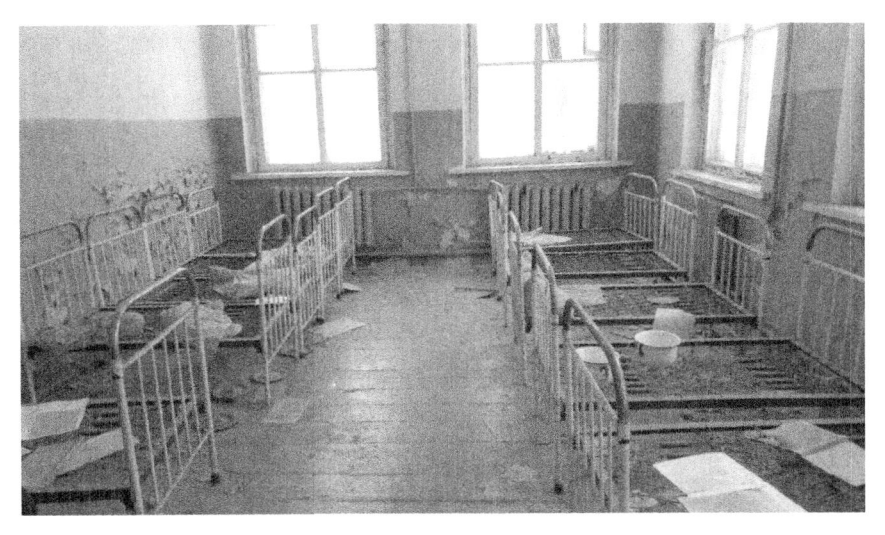

9: Bedroom in Kopachi kindergarten

Of all the impressions of this trip, the rooms full of small cribs are among the most memorable. In the large, light-flooded dormitories, the wireframes of the beds stand side by side, sometimes singly, sometimes in two tiers. The mattresses are completely missing; only occasionally we find the remains of a few pillows, blankets, and chamber pots. A shiver runs down our spines, given the inconceivable suffering that fell upon the nearly 15,000 children in the area due to the accident. Most of them had surely envisioned a future with their families in the flourishing economic region at that time. The sight of children's toys, dolls, and cuddly toys left behind intensifies the oppressive feeling.

As exciting and impressive as the visit to the restricted zone had been so far, we had not yet seen anything of the actual destination of our trip. This was soon to change on the drive from Kopachi to Pripyat. The Geiger counter now rattles on almost continuously here in the core of the death zone. Without this alarm signal, we would probably not even be aware of the special situation we are in. During our stay of just a few hours, we had almost become familiar with the circumstances so that the drive through the open terrain felt almost like an ordinary winter excursion along a lonely country road.

Suddenly, a large plant appears on the horizon between dense fog. Our hearts beat faster when we saw the Chernobyl nuclear power plant for the first time, or what was left of it. At first, it is not clear to us which part of the building is in front of us. The nuclear power plant itself, as we had learned, consisted of several individual reactors, two of which were still under construction at the time of the catastrophe, and one of the completed reactors was still in operation for years into the 1990s. Kateryna enlightens us that the building complex we can see is the construction site of reactors 5 and 6.

10: Unfinished construction site of reactors 5 and 6

The facility itself is huge and, in addition to several buildings, consists of a dense network of chimneys, power lines, and construction cranes. From the outside, the buildings remind us of unimpressive factory halls. We get out at a vantage point and try to capture the scene photographically. Although it's pretty much noon, the sun seems to have all but disappeared through the dense fog. With temperatures as low as 5 °F, it has become bitterly cold. Thickly wrapped in our warm winter clothes, we hastily take a photo before continuing our drive to the city of Pripyat. On the way, we catch our first glimpse of the disaster reactor 4, which is shielded by a semicircular dome in the style of an airplane hangar. It won't be long before we are allowed to approach it within a few hundred feet.

Exploring the ghost town of Pripyat

Pripyat is the place with the shortest distance to the nuclear power plant. There is also one of the most contaminated regions in the world at its entrance: The Red Forest. The radioactive fallout here caused parts of the forest to die. As part of the clean-up effort, attempts were made to remove the contamination by cutting down the dead trees and burying the trunks on the site. The leaves of the remaining trees turned copper-red due to the radiation, giving the forest its name. Visitors to the red forest here are exposed to radiation levels of up to 20 microsieverts per hour, which is 100 times the naturally occurring radiation. While the plant life in large parts of the restricted area has recovered very well and, in some cases, appears more magnificent today than it did under human influence, attempts to reforest the Red Forest have so far been unsuccessful.

11: Pripyat town sign

Prypyat was still a young city at the time of the reactor accident. It was founded only in 1970 as a housing estate for the nuclear power plant workers, and in the following 16 years, it grew into a medium-sized city with 50,000 inhabitants. Due to the perfect economic situation, which the nuclear power plant generated as the largest employer in the region, the town became a modern settlement for the time. It had every imaginable amenity, such as a sports stadium, a swimming pool, and even an amusement park. Pripyat was, therefore, an attractive place to live, especially for young families with children.

After the accident, a full 36 hours passed before Pripyat residents were informed of the high radiation levels and subsequently evacuated. As a result, the residents were unknowingly exposed to very high radiation levels, and many of them continued to suffer from late effects for years afterward. When the political leadership finally decided to move forward with the evacuation, the process was carried out by 1,200 buses in a period of just two and a half hours. Residents left their town believing that it would be only a short-term retreat and that they would be able to return to their homes a few days later after the clean-up was completed. Therefore, they packed only the essentials and left their familiar homes almost fully equipped. In the time that has passed since then, the town has been completely looted by the illegal settlers who stayed in the exclusion zone despite the radiation. Contaminated valuables were stolen without thinking about the dangers involved. Boards and wood paneling were removed from homes and used as construction or firewood. The remaining personal belongings and furnishings are still in the ghost town today.

Since 2017, visiting the buildings in the city of Pripyat has been strictly prohibited by the administration of the exclusion zone. The buildings were not further secured in the decades after the disaster and are structurally in such a poor condition due to the long shutdown that some of them are in danger of collapse. Patrolling police officers control the compliance with this prohibition and intervene with strict measures in case of violations. During our visit, we still have the opportunity to take a look inside the buildings. In the meantime, we have switched the Geiger counters, which permanently sound the alarm in the most inner circle of the restricted zone, to mute mode. The thought of switching off the alarm, which should save one's life in an emergency because it is now considered annoying, seems foolish to us at first. Curiosity about the inner workings of the buildings is greater, so we don't spend much time on this thought and rather set off.

The first thing we catch is a brief glimpse of a shopping mall. There is no sign here of the fact that the city flourished economically in the 1980s due to the nuclear power plant as a significant employer in the region and that the up-and-coming city offered some amenities and luxuries. The stores were looted long ago. The building materials that could still be used elsewhere have been dismantled and used for wild settlements. What remained was rubble, shards, and junk, as well as the slowly decaying building fabric.

12: Looted shopping center in Pripyat

On foot, we now march to the amusement park of Pripyat, which we are most excited to visit. The amusement park offered a Ferris wheel, a bumper car, and a merry-go-round, almost everything that one wanted from a modern amusement park at that time. Especially the empty Ferris wheel with its yellow cabins has become a kind of sad landmark of Chernobyl and, next to the containment, is probably one of the most frequently photographed structures of the exclusion zone. Among other things, it has also gained fame through its depiction in various computer games.

13: The Ferris wheel in the amusement park of Pripyat

Apart from the tramp of our footsteps in the snow, nothing can be heard as we slowly move through the amusement park in our small group. The amusement park is located in an extensive area that nature has now reclaimed to a considerable extent. Where there used to be wide open spaces for visitors, there are now trees as tall as houses. The amusement rides stand out like foreign bodies in the otherwise untouched winter landscape. Only the gray concrete of the surrounding buildings reminds us that we are still in the middle of the city. We are particularly impressed by the quiet atmosphere around the amusement park also because of its bitter circumstances. The attractions could never really be used by crowds of carefree children. The amusement park's opening was planned for May 01, 1986, but a few days earlier, the catastrophe ruined these plans.

14: Playground overgrown with trees

Crossing the soccer field, we continue towards the Pripyat school. Only the remains of the soccer stand suggest that what can now be interpreted as a city park or forest is actually the city's soccer stadium.

The entrance to the school is hidden by overgrown shrubs, making it difficult to see at first. We approach the building cautiously, pausing briefly to listen for sounds that might indicate the presence of more people. Except for the whistling of the wind, we hear nothing from the building. We look at each other briefly, nod silently to each other, and then enter the former school. Only a little light penetrates the first floor through the shadows of the wildly risen trees. Here, as well, leaves and dust have blown in through the partially open windows. The hallways appear bare and wide due to the lack of interior furnishings. The blue paint is peeling off the walls in large shreds. Electric cables hanging from the ceiling and water pipes protruding from the wall form the remains of hastily dismantled lamps and radiators. We move slowly through the corridors, passing rotten wooden frames and rusty metal grates, and finally reach a large room, the sight of which takes our breath away for a moment. The room is littered with hundreds, if not thousands, of used gas masks. The masks are made of brown rubber and have a small round glass viewing window for each eye. For the air supply, a filter insert with a metallic cap is attached to a flexible tube. The sight makes us, who have had no contact with gas masks in everyday life and only know them from dramatic films about nuclear, biological, or chemical attacks, shudder. We inspect the room with an alarming feeling. In addition to the remains of the equipment, the horrible thought that we might also come across the dead bodies of its wearer's creeps into our minds.

15: Gas masks in the basement of the Pripyat school

We are quite relieved when we reach the actual classrooms of the school on the floor above. The rooms here are already much brighter, and also the familiar-looking furnishings of the classrooms reassure us. Although there is quite a bit of chaos in the classrooms, we can still recognize very well the individual rows of seats with the school desks and the corresponding chairs. Scattered everywhere are paper pages faded by the sun, individual pieces of paper, and even entire textbooks. The books are amazingly well preserved and even still readable. Besides many Russian texts, we even discover a German novel. According to research after our return, it was the novel "Die Aula" by Hermann Kant, published in 1965, which traces the history of the workers' and farmers' faculties in the German Democratic Republic. We try not to touch anything and to leave all objects unchanged as a glimpse into the past, as they have been since the evacuation of Pripyat more than three decades ago.

16: Classroom in the school of Pripyat

We next reach a huge hall. Judging by the rusted iron struts on the ceiling, which is at least two stories high, this could very well be a factory hall. However, the wooden floor laid throughout, and the basketball hoop on the wall tells us that we are looking at a sports hall. Considering the decades of vacancy and the fact that the hall was neither heated nor protected from moisture during this time, the hall is still in very good condition except for the influence of natural weathering. The wooden floor is cracked in a few rotten places, but there are no signs of vandalism. We are particularly impressed by the view from the spacious window front on the left side of the hall, from which the yellow Ferris wheel can be seen. Wistfully, we think of how beautiful life would have been in the city if the catastrophe had never occurred.

Our last stop in Pripyat is a place that has become one of the sad landmarks of the city, and that should not be missed on any tour: the Pripyat swimming pool. Like the sports hall before, the swimming pool is in an exceptionally well-preserved condition. The two diving towers, the ceiling-high window fronts, the entry ladders, and the small gallery above the pool stand ready for use in front of us. The pool, which slopes steeply from a shallow non-swimmer area to the deep landing area of the diving towers, is still almost entirely covered with small, square, slightly yellowed white tiles.

17: Pripyat swimming pool

After the disaster, the pool continued to operate for a total of ten more years for liquidators and workers at the remaining nuclear power plant before it was closed in 1996 following safety concerns.

Lunch break in the Chernobyl canteen

Due to the many exciting impressions, the time flies by, and so it doesn't bother us at all that we don't leave for lunch until around 1:30 p.m. The touching pictures still occupy all of us and make sure that our appetite does not really arise. The prospect of feeding our bodies in one of the most contaminated places in the world does not help much either. On the other hand, these circumstances also make us curious, and so lunch, without having thought about it beforehand, also turns out to be an exciting program item of this trip. The special thing about this meal is that we ate it in the middle of the exclusion zone in the same canteen where the workers of the nuclear power plant and the employees of the administration of the exclusion zone go every day.

We first have to pass through a security check to enter the canteen, where we are examined for radiation residues. To do this, we enter one by one a gray detector that reminds us of the body scanner at modern airports. We stand upright in the apparatus, place our hands at about chest level on two measuring plates, and within a few seconds, we receive the positive signal that we are allowed to pass through the canteen. The dining hall is already less crowded at this point, so we quickly find a free table and quickly pick up our meal at the food counter. The menu consists of the traditional soup borscht, a piece of fish with egg noodles, and Ukrainian pancakes filled with cottage cheese. The food is very tasty, and the amount of portion is sufficient in any case. Kateryna also assures us that the meal is, of course, healthy, as the ingredients are freshly imported from outside the zone. By the way, in the canteen, the radiation level is not higher than in a big western city. Only after we come to rest for a moment in the warm room, the morning's efforts become noticeable. By then, we had already been on our feet for 8 hours, roaming the exclusion zone area at temperatures of 5 °F on our short sightseeing tours and processing the strong impressions of the morning. Even more, we now enjoy the fact that we can take a short break and recharge our energy with lunch.

The sarcophagus above the damaged reactor core

After lunch, we leave for the place we have been looking forward to all day. We will now approach the disaster reactor up to a few hundred feet. We park in the immediate neighborhood of the center of the disaster, on the side of the road that leads through the vast area of the nuclear power plant, and enter the small square in front of the entrance gates. Our eyes are fixed firmly on the protective shell that replaces the shielding hastily concreted over after the accident as a long-term solution. Beneath the sarcophagus, officially called the New Safe Confinement, an unimaginable 96 percent of the radioactive debris from the reactor core still lies dormant. Knowing that thousands of workers from all over the world participated in the construction work on-site for several months and remained unharmed takes away the fear that shoots up inside us at the first glimpse of the sarcophagus.

18: Sarcophagus over the accident reactor 4

At first glance, the protective shell appears to be an ordinary airplane hangar from the outside, which is without a doubt an impressive construction from a technical point of view. With its height of 358 feet, it surpasses the Statue of Liberty and, with a width of over 820 feet, offers enough space to accommodate the Colosseum in Rome. In addition, it is protected for at least 100 years against all imaginable external influences and natural disasters. Thanks to the protective shell, we are not exposed to any higher levels of radiation in the immediate surroundings of the reactor core than, for example, in the ghost town of Pripyat.

However, this was not always the case: the old sarcophagus, initially installed as a temporary structure after the disaster, was never designed as a long-term solution. Over the years, the steel girders that were used increasingly rusted, putting the structure at risk of collapsing at some point. In addition, the old sarcophagus had also leaked, allowing radiation to escape and water to enter the damaged reactor, which then leaked contaminated into the ground. Before the New Safe Confinement was put into operation, the radiation level on-site was so high that the workers involved in the construction could not be expected to stay there for any length of time. Therefore, the protective shell was erected about 700 feet away from the accident reactor and slowly slid over the old concrete structure on rails in November 2016. This makes the new protective shelter the largest mobile structure in the world.

We are a little proud when we learn from Kateryna that we were probably one of the first visitors to see the massive structure with our own eyes during our visit to Chernobyl just a few days after the inauguration of the new sarcophagus.

The departure from the exclusion zone

Up to this point, everything had gone well on our tour of the restricted area, all participants were fine, and the original excitement and worries had given way to a feeling of consternation and overwhelm. Now only one last car ride separates us from the supposedly safe area outside Chernobyl.

It is already getting dusk as we take the road out towards the checkpoint. We drive along untouched forests, where nature has been able to develop unhindered for decades. Suddenly the driver draws our attention to a rare discovery. On the side of the road, we spot a group of three wild horses in the light of the headlights. Our sighting is of Przewalski's horses, a nearly extinct wild horse that has been reintroduced into the restricted area and is now reproducing there without the influence of humans. This sight makes us wonder: was the departure of humankind possibly even a benefit for the flora and fauna in the region? Is the presence of humans perhaps even more damaging than a nuclear disaster of such magnitude? The long-term consequences on nature are still disputed today. The disaster initially ended fatally for the majority of animals in the immediate vicinity around the nuclear power plant. The remaining animals continued to suffer from reduced reproductive capacity, abnormalities and mutations, and increased mortality for years. In the decades that followed, the animals seemed to have developed a resistance to the radiation. Without the threatening influence of humans on the habitat, the population recovered, so that threatened animal species such as wolves, elk, bison, and brown bears, as well as rare bird species, are now once again firmly established in the restricted area.

Before passing through the checkpoint, we have to undergo another security check. This is to prevent radioactive residues from the exclusion zone from being carried into the populated country. While our minibus is examined outside by a militia officer with a radiation detector, we cross the border through a body scanner in an administrative building. Kateryna had warned us in advance not to take souvenirs from the restricted zone. In addition to the harmful consequences for our health, this can sometimes lead to a refusal to leave the restricted zone and to a quarantine order if the measured values are too high. Nervousness spreads among us. No one wants the experience of being the only one left in the restricted zone. We meticulously stamp the dirt off our shoes and wipe the snow off our jackets. With a queasy feeling in our stomachs, we enter the detector one by one, and after a few agonizing seconds, we are released one by one into freedom.

Over the course of the day, we absorbed a total of about 3 microsieverts of radiation during our visit to the restricted area. This represented at most a quarter of the radiation we were exposed to during our flight to Ukraine. The big difference here is that normally one is not even aware of the exposure to cosmic radiation when flying and therefore does not worry about it. Also, compared to the radiation exposure, which one typically takes in during the year and which amounts to 2100 microsieverts on average, the stay in Chernobyl is hardly significant.

Even though there were no health risks at any time, we and our family and friends are nevertheless relieved that we are well and richer in a valuable experience after our visit to Chernobyl.

A day in the Chernobyl exclusion zone - My personal conclusion

The trip to the Chernobyl exclusion zone was one of the most impressive experiences I have ever had. Even years later, I am moved by the history of this place and the fate of its people.

The tour itself was professionally organized throughout, from departure in the morning to return in Kiev in the evening. We felt safe at all times under the care of our driver and guide. The well-founded background knowledge about the individual scenes helped us better understand the events on site and helped us grasp the initially abstract extent of the catastrophe.

During the day, an unbelievable number of impressions and feelings flooded in:
- Anticipation of being allowed to visit this extraordinary place
- Excitement about the unknown that awaited us in the Chernobyl "death zone."
- Apprehension about the still-present dangers of the invisible and tasteless, and odorless radiation
- Curiosity and desire for exploration during our independent investigations
- Fear and discomfort in the face of the eerie atmosphere in the abandoned buildings

- Helplessness at the thought of the ineffectiveness of the possible countermeasures because of the superiority of the radiation in terms of radiation intensity, wide local distribution, and temporal permanence
- Consternation at the thought of the fates of the emergency workers, families, and children
- Confidence and hope that nature is slowly recovering and that the flora and fauna in the restricted area have meanwhile found a retreat from humans
- Thoughtfulness, whether our visit counts as a curious onlooker or as an educational excursion
- Gratitude that we are doing well and have so far been spared catastrophes of this magnitude

This emotional experience and the opportunity to see the sites of the events with our own eyes ensured that this sad chapter in the history of industrialization came alive for us and was thus permanently branded into our memory.

I would like to recommend the tour to the Chernobyl exclusion zone to anyone who wants to see the historical events for themselves and see the effects of the nuclear catastrophe with their own eyes. However, the main focus of such a trip should always be historical interest and remembrance of the victims of this disaster. Even though our trip started out of a sense of adventure and the drive to bring home exciting stories and tales, Chernobyl has become a place of remembrance for me after this trip. It stands as a memorial to a cautious approach to new technology and the forces of nature.

Considering the increasing popularity of Chernobyl as a travel destination, I wish that every visitor would bring the respect to their trip that this place and its former inhabitants deserve.

19: Entrance to the Chernobyl exclusion zone

20: Abandoned building in Pripyat

21: Toy left behind

22: Vehicles for the clean-up

23: Overgrown entrance to the school of Pripyat

24: Pripyat sports hall

Bonus chapter: The secret radar station Duga-1

On the way back from the reactor sarcophagus to the border checkpoint, we stop at another facility that is located in the exclusion zone but has only an indirect connection with the Chernobyl nuclear power plant.

Via a narrow access road in the middle of a dense coniferous forest, we reach a military area, which was masked as a youth hostel in the times of the Soviet Union. After a short walk, we realize that the object, which is classified as top secret, is a huge radar installation. The Duga-1 radar system (often mistakenly called Duga-3) consists of a total of 50 receiving antennas, each with 44 arms and thousands and thousands of metal wires. The transmission towers reach a height of up to 500 feet. The entire system is an unimaginable 2,500 feet wide.

25: Radar system Duga-1

The facility became known as the "Russian Woodpecker" because the rapid, knocking sound of the shortwave signal heard on radio frequencies worldwide was reminiscent of a woodpecker in the forest. The Duga facilities, of which there were two more in southern Ukraine, were part of the Soviet missile defense system during its operational period from 1976 to 1989. Because of its considerable size and associated capability, the facility was able to detect launches of missiles within a radius of up to 6,200 miles. It thus covered most of the European and American airspace.

The close proximity to the Chernobyl nuclear power plant had two major advantages for Duga-1. On the one hand, the short connection ensured a round-the-clock power supply to this enormous plant, and on the other hand, the area around the power plant was well secured anyway and hardly accessible to foreign visitors. The secrecy meant that hardly anyone in the civilian population, and certainly no one abroad, knew of the existence of these facilities.

It was not until the reactor disaster that information about the radar system became public. This also resolved the wild theories about the purpose of the "Russian Woodpecker," which ranged from influencing the weather to mind control of the Soviet population. Thanks to the evacuation after the accident and the observance of the exclusion zone in the following decades, the radar installation still exists today and can be visited.

During our visit to the Duga-1 radar facility, we are particularly amazed by the immense financial and technological expenditures that both sides took on during the Cold War. The size of the facility alone is impressive and can hardly be represented accurately on photos. From our point of view, Duga-1 is definitely worth a visit.

Frequently Asked Questions (FAQ)

Is a trip to Chernobyl safe?
Based on the absorbed radiation during our stay in the Chernobyl exclusion zone, the trip can be classified as harmless to health. Exaggeratedly, one could say that due to the natural radiation when flying, the most dangerous part of our trip to Chernobyl was the outbound and return flights by plane.

Nevertheless, the risk of injury when entering buildings that are now heavily dilapidated should not be underestimated. The building materials have been exposed to the elements unprotected by decades of vacancy. Caution is especially needed with rotten wooden floors and with protruding, sharp-edged metal parts. If you are aware of the risk and move carefully through the area as an averagely fit person, the risk is acceptable from our point of view.

Kiev, the city we visited, and the area around Chernobyl are considered politically stable. We were always treated politely and courteously, both by the locals and by the security forces, so that we felt safe all around.

Approximately how much radiation does a person absorb when visiting the restricted area?
In most places within the exclusion zone, the radiation measured in the air is approximately at the same level as in many well-known cities worldwide. In some cases, we even measured values that were below the average value of 0.24 microsieverts per hour for natural

radiation exposure in Germany. Significantly greater danger comes from so-called hotspots, i.e., local places with particularly high radiation. Radiated objects should also not be touched under any circumstances.

Over the course of the day, we absorbed a total of about 3 microsieverts of radiation during our visit to the restricted area. For comparison: a short-haul flight exposes the body to about 20 microsieverts, a long-haul flight to over 60 microsieverts, and a chest X-ray examination to up to 400 microsieverts. Compared to the radiation exposure typically absorbed during a year, which averages 2.1 millisieverts (equivalent to 2100 microsieverts), the stay in Chernobyl is hardly significant.

How much does a visit to the Chernobyl exclusion zone cost?

The cost of visiting Chernobyl consists of the cost of travel to and from the site (often by air), the cost of accommodation before and after the tour, and the cost of the actual tour of the exclusion zone. Unfortunately, since the price of airline tickets depends on the timing of the trip and the particular departure airport, it is impossible to answer this question. However, as soon as one reaches Ukraine, the prices are on a favorable level from a Western perspective. Private apartments in the city center start at 35 US dollars per night, and a normal lunch for two people (starter, drinks, and main course) costs the equivalent of no more than 12 US dollars.

The prices for the excursion to Chernobyl differ slightly depending on the provider and are about 100 US dollars for the one-day tour and about 250 US dollars per person for the two-day tour. In our case, the rental fee for the Geiger counter (10 US dollars) and the flat rate for lunch (8 US dollars) had to be added.

How do the various tours differentiate themselves?
In general, we distinguish between one-day and multi-day tours. When choosing a tour, we believe that you should make sure that you visit Kopachi, Chernobyl, and Pripyat and that you have the opportunity to see the sarcophagus from a distance of only 1,000 feet. On the multi-day tour, you will stay in a hotel inside the exclusion zone and have the opportunity to visit other interesting places for which there is not enough time on the 1-day tour (e.g., an exhibition on radioactively contaminated vehicles, other places along the Pripyat River, etc.) as well as meet the locals of the exclusion zone in person. If revisiting Chernobyl, I would definitely choose the more extensive 2-day tour.

In addition, some thematic tours deal more intensively with, for example, Soviet history or the military occurrences around the radar stations.

How close can you get to the accident reactor?
During a normal tour, the accident reactor is viewed from a small square in front of the entrance gates of the nuclear power plant from a distance of about 1,000 feet. Thereby, you have a very good view of the new sarcophagus ("New Safe Confinement"), which is supposed to shield the destroyed reactor.

According to reports on the Internet, it is now even possible to visit the control room of the accident reactor, which was closed to ordinary tourists until now, on special guided tours. A visit takes place in white suits, with helmet and breathing apparatus, and lasts no longer than 5 minutes.

Should you borrow a Geiger counter?

Absolutely yes! With the help of a Geiger counter, it is possible to measure the invisible, tasteless and odorless radiation. Only when the radiation was shown on display did we really become aware of the ever-present danger. Furthermore, it gave us the opportunity to search for evidence even more intensively and to compare the different locations at different distances from the accident reactor. To put it in the words of liquidator, environmentalist, and book author Sergii Mirnyi: "Going to the Chernobyl zone without a dosimeter is like going blindfolded on a normal tour."

Should you have lunch in Chernobyl?

Absolutely yes! With arrival and departure from Kiev, you are almost 12 hours on the road with the group, of which you spend almost 8 hours in the exclusion zone. Due to the excitement, we didn't immediately realize how exhausting the day was with all the little visits on foot in the fresh air and all the strong impressions. All the more we enjoyed that we could take a little break and strengthen ourselves with lunch. The food was quite tasty and, of course, healthy, as the ingredients are freshly imported from outside the zone. In the canteen itself, the radiation level is no higher than in any large western city as well.

Moreover, after our return, our story about having lunch with the workers of the Chernobyl nuclear power plant in their canteen was always taken as something special.

What is the best time to visit Chernobyl?

In general, Ukraine is very easy to visit all year round. The travel period with the highest chances of good weather is in the months from May to September. Although the warmest temperatures are from June to August, they also receive the most rain. Visiting Chernobyl is possible both in the summer months and in the winter months. While in the summer months, the wild shrubs and trees are in full bloom, it is impressive to see how much nature has taken back the habitat in the exclusion zone. On the other hand, during our visit to Chernobyl in mid-December, the black and white landscape of snow, bare trees, and gray buildings added to the gloomy atmosphere of the abandoned villages, creating a very special mood in us. However, in the months of December and January, you have to be prepared for low temperatures of up to minus 4 °F when choosing your clothes.

Do people still live in the restricted area?

On the territory of the exclusion zone in Ukraine and Belarus, there are still several hundred illegal settlers, the so-called "Samosely" (translated roughly: self-settlers). These are mainly elderly people who either refused to leave their homes during the evacuation or have since returned. Because they are providing themselves with food from private farms, they are exposed to much higher radiation levels, in contrast to the Chernobyl employees who obtain their food from outside the exclusion zone.

Who is not allowed to enter the restricted zone?
Access to the restricted zone is generally open to persons over 18 years of age. As further distances are covered on foot throughout the day, and some exposed areas require surefootedness, the tour is only recommended for people with average physical fitness and no health restrictions. Access to the restricted area is also not granted to pregnant women for safety reasons.

What should I definitely not do?
A visit to the Chernobyl exclusion zone is only safe if you follow the guides' instructions exactly. On the one hand, this applies to the dress code (sturdy shoes, long trousers) and, on the other hand, to the important rules of conduct on-site. These refer to staying together within the group, staying on marked trails, and not touching materials and objects in the restricted zone.

Under no circumstances should you try to take home souvenirs from the exclusion zone. This applies equally to stones, plants, and other objects. While the radiation in the air in Chernobyl is no longer higher than in many metropolises worldwide, the radiation exposure on objects can quickly be hundreds or thousands of times higher. In addition to the harmful consequences for health when taking souvenirs, this can lead to conflicts when leaving the exclusion zone, as every guest is checked for radiation residues on the way back. If the values are too high, departure from the exclusion zone can sometimes even be refused, and quarantine may be ordered.

Acknowledgements

I would like to take this opportunity to thank the people who supported me in the creation of this book.

A special thanks go to my brother Tim, who accompanied the creation of the travelogue for weeks and critically questioned my explanations. Thanks to his attention to detail and his passion for historical background, the travelogue has become richer by many exciting facts. Thank you very much for supporting me at any time with words and actions.

Furthermore, I would like to thank my girlfriend Regina from the bottom of my heart for the encouragement and the necessary space that made this project possible. Your patience with me is unique. I am especially happy that we share the love of adventure in special places. Our travels together will certainly provide plenty of material for new stories in the future.

In memory of the fellow travelers on the journey to Chernobyl

                              Clemens

                              Lukas

                              Marcel

                              Marten

Printed in Great Britain
by Amazon